COLLECTOR'S ITEM

COLLECTOR'S ITEM

by Evelyn E. Smith

Being trapped in the steaming h–l of Venus is no excuse for forgetting one's manners—but anyone abducted, marooned, tricked, kept from tea might well crack under the strain!

"What I should like to know," Professor Bernardi said, gazing pensively after the lizard-man as he bore the shrieking form of Miss Anspacher off in his scaly arms, "is whether he is planning to eat her or make love to her. Because, in the latter instance, I'm not sure we should interfere. It may be her only chance."

"Carl!" his wife cried indignantly. "That's a horrid thing to say! You must rescue her at once!"

"Oh, I suppose so," he said, then gave his wife a nasty little grin that he knew would irritate her. "It isn't that she's unattractive, my dear, in case you hadn't noticed, though she's pretty well past the bloom of youth—"

"*Will* you stop making leering noises and go save her or *not?*"

"I was coming to that. It's just that she persists in using her Ph.D. as a club to beat men into respectful pulps. Men don't like being beaten into respectful pulps, whether by a man or a woman. Now if she'd only learned that other people have feelings—"

"If you don't stop lecturing and go, I will!" his wife threatened.

"All right, all right," he said wearily. "Come on, Mortland."

*

The two scientists slogged through the steamy, odorous jungle of Venus and soon reached the lizard-man, who, weighed down by his captive, had not been able to travel as fast.

"You blast him," the professor told Mortland. "Try not to hit Miss Anspacher, if you can manage it."

COLLECTOR'S ITEM

"Er—I've never fired one of these things before," Mortland said. "Can't stand having my eardrums blasted. However, here goes." He pointed his weapon at the lizardlike creature in a gingerly manner. "Ah—hands up," he ordered. "Only fair to give the—well, blighter a sporting chance," he explained to Professor Bernardi.

To their amazement, the lizard-man promptly dropped Miss Anspacher into the lavender-colored mud and put up his hands. Miss Anspacher gave an indignant yelp.

"Seems intelligent in spite of the kidnaping," Mortland commented. "But how does he happen to understand English? We're the only expedition ever to have reached Venus . . . that I know of, anyway." He and the professor stared at each other in consternation. "There may have been a secret expedition previously and perhaps they left a—a base or something, which would explain why—"

"If you two oafs would stop speculating, you might help me out of here!" Miss Anspacher remarked in her customary snappish tone. Professor Bernardi leaped forward to obey. "You don't have to pull quite so hard! I haven't taken root yet!" She came out of the mud with a sound like two whales kissing. She brushed hopelessly at her once-white blouse and shorts. "Oh, dear, I look a mess!"

Professor Bernardi did not comment, being engaged in slapping at a small winged creature—about the size of a bluejay, but looking like a cross between a bat and a mosquito—that seemed interested in taking a bite out of him. It escaped his flapping hand and flew to the top of Mortland's sun helmet, where it glared at the professor.

"Since you seem to understand English," Miss Anspacher said to the lizard-man through a mouthful of hairpins, "perhaps you will be so kind as to explain the meaning of this outrage?"

"I was smitten," the alien replied suavely. "Passion made me forget myself."

Professor Bernardi looked thoughtfully at him. "A prior expedition isn't the answer. It wouldn't have troubled to educate you so thoroughly. Therefore, the explanation is that you pick up English by reading our minds. Correct?"

The lizard-man turned an embarrassed olive. "Yes."

*

Now that he was able to give the creature a more thorough inspection, Bernardi saw that he really didn't look too much like a lizard. He definitely appeared to be wearing clothes of some kind, which, in the Venusian heat, indicated a particularly refined degree of civilization—unless, of course, the squamous skin protected him from the heat as well as the humidity.

More than that, though, he was humanoid in almost a Hollywood way. He had a particularly fine profile and an athletic physique, which, oddly, his scales seemed to enhance, much like a movie idol dressed in fine-meshed Medieval armor. Naturally, he had a tail, but it was as well proportioned as a kangaroo's, though shorter and more graceful, and it struck Professor Bernardi as a particularly handsome and useful gadget.

For one thing, the people from Earth were standing uncomfortably in the slippery mud, while the lizard-man was using his tail much in the fashion of a spectator stool, leaning back against it almost in a sitting position, with his armor-shod feet supporting him comfortably. For another, the tail undoubtedly served for balance and the added push of a walking stick and perhaps for swift attack or getaway. Very practical and attractive, the professor concluded—too bad Man had relinquished his tail when climbing down from the trees.

COLLECTOR'S ITEM

"Thank you," the saurian said with uneasy modesty, looking at him. "Good of you to think so. You are a fairly intelligent species, aren't you?"

"Fairly," the professor acknowledged, preoccupied with a clever idea. Perhaps existence on Venus wasn't going to be as unpleasant as he had anticipated. "From reading my mind, you know what this blaster can do, don't you?"

"I'm afraid so."

"Then you know what I expect of you?"

"Yes, sahib. I'se comin', massa. To hear is to obey, effendi." The creature turned and went briskly back toward the camp, leaving the others to stumble after him.

Mrs. Bernardi gave a shriek as his handsome scaled form emerged from the greenish-white underbrush, haloed in luminous yellow mist. Algol, the ship's cat, prudently took sanctuary behind her, then peered out to see what was going on and whether there was likely to be anything in it for him.

"This is our native bearer," Professor Bernardi explained as the three scientists burst out of the jungle.

"My name is Jrann-Pttt." The creature bowed low. "At your service, madame."

"Oh, Carl!" Mrs. Bernardi clapped her hands. "He's just perfect! So thoughtful of you to find one that speaks English! I do hope you can cook, Pitt?"

"I will do my best, madame."

*

Algol daintily picked his way through the mud toward the saurian, sniffed him with judicial deliberation; then, deciding that anyone who smelled so much like the better class of fish must be All Right, rubbed against his legs.

8

"Well," remarked Miss Anspacher, using the side of the spaceship as a mirror by which to redden her somewhat prissy lips, "that makes it practically unanimous, doesn't it?"

"All except Professor Bernardi," said Jrann-Pttt, looking at the scientist with what might have been a smile. "He doesn't like me."

"I see that your telepathic powers are not quite accurate," the professor returned. "I do not dislike you; I distrust you."

"The fact that the two terms are not entirely synonymous in your language would argue a certain degree of incipient civilization," the lizard-man observed.

"You know, Carl," Mrs. Bernardi whispered, "he has an awfully funny way of talking, for a native."

"Frankly I don't like this at all, Professor," Captain Greenfield said, mopping his brow with a limp handkerchief. "If I hadn't been off looking for a better berth for the ship—all this mud worries me—this'd never have happened."

"You mean you would have let the lizard get away with Miss Anspacher?"

The big man's face flushed crimson. "I don't think that's funny, Professor."

Bernardi quickly changed the subject, for he realized that the captain, being by far the most muscular of the party, was not a man to trifle with. "Tell me, Greenfield, did you succeed in finding a better spot for the ship? I must admit I'm worried about that mud myself."

"Only remotely dry spot around is an outcropping 'bout two kilometers away," Greenfield said grudgingly. He shifted his camp stool in a futile search for shade. Even though the sun never penetrated the thick layer of clouds, the yellow light diffused through them was blinding. "Might be big enough, but it's not level. Could blast it smooth, but that'd take at least a week—Earth time."

Bernardi pulled his damp shirt away from his body. "Well, I daresay we'll be all right where we are, if we're not assailed by any violent forces of nature. On Earth, this might be a monsoon climate."

"If you ask me, that monster is more of a danger than any monsoon."

Bernardi sighed. Although by far the most competent officer available for the job of spaceship captain, Greenfield was not quite the man he would have chosen to be his associate for months on end. Still, beggars—as Miss Anspacher might have eloquently put it—could not be choosers. "What makes you say that?" he asked, trying to set an example of tolerance.

"Don't like the idea of him cooking for us," the captain said stubbornly. "Might poison us all in our beds."

"Well, don't eat in your bed," suggested Mortland, strolling out of the airlock in the company of the cat. Algol, however, finding that the spot beside the captain's camp stool was as dry as anything could be on Venus, decided to turn back.

*

"The difficulty is easily overcome, Captain," the professor said, still holding on to his patience. "You can continue to cook your own meals from the tinned and packaged foods on board ship. The rest of us will eat fresh native foods prepared by Jrann-Pttt."

"But why," Miss Anspacher interrupted as she emerged from the airlock with a large cast-iron skillet, "should you think Jrann-Pttt wants to poison us?"

Both men rose from their stools. "Stands to reason he'd consider us his enemies, Miss Anspacher," the captain said. "After all, we—as a group, that is—captured him."

"Hired him," Professor Bernardi contradicted. "I've telepathically arranged to pay him an adequate salary. In goods, of course; I don't suppose our money would be of much use to him. And I think he's rather glad of the chance to hang around and observe us conveniently."

"Observe us!" Greenfield exclaimed. "You mean he's spying out the land for an attack? Let's prepare our defenses at once!"

"I doubt if that's what he has in mind," Professor Bernardi said judiciously.

"He may be staying because he wants to be near me," Miss Anspacher blurted. Overcome by this unmaidenly admission, she reddened and rushed from them, calling, "Yoo-hoo, Jrann-Pttt! Here is the frying pan!" Algol woke up instantly and followed her. "Frying" was one of the more important words in his vocabulary.

Captain Greenfield stared across the clearing after them, then turned back to Bernardi with a frown. "I don't like to see one of our girls mixed up with a lizard—and a foreign lizard at that." But his face too clearly betrayed a personal resentment.

"Don't tell me you have a—a fondness for Miss Anspacher, Captain," Professor Bernardi exclaimed, genuinely surprised. Undeniably Miss Anspacher—although no longer in her first youth—was a handsome woman, but he would not have expected her somewhat cerebral type to appeal to the captain. On the other hand, she was the only unattached woman in the party and they were a long way from home.

Greenfield picked a fleck of dried violet mud from the side of the ship and avoided Bernardi's eye. "One of the reasons I came along," he said almost bashfully. "Thought I'd have the chance to be alone with her now and again and impress her with, with. . . . "

"Your sterling qualities?" Bernardi suggested.

11

COLLECTOR'S ITEM

The captain flashed him a glance of mingled gratitude and resentment. "And now this damned lizard has to come along!"

"Cheer up, Captain," said the professor. "I'll back you against a lizard any time."

*

Although the long twilight of Venus had deepened into night and it could never really be cool there by terrestrial standards, the temperature was almost comfortable. Everything was quite black, except for the pallid purple campfire glowing through the darkness; the clouds that perpetually covered the surface of the planet prevented even the light of the stars from reaching it.

"Tell me more about the cross-versus the parallel-cousin relationships in your culture, Jrann-Pttt," Miss Anspacher breathed, wriggling her camp stool closer to the saurian's. "Anthropology is a great hobby of mine, you know. How do your people feel about exogamy?"

"I'm afraid I'm rather exhausted, dear lady," he said, using one arm to mask a yawn, and one to surreptitiously wave away the saurian head that was peering out of the underbrush. "I shouldn't like to give a scientist like yourself any misinformation that might become a matter of record."

"Of course not," she murmured. "You're so considerate."

*

A pale face appeared in the firelight like some weird creature of darkness. Terrestrial and extraterrestrial both started. "Miss Anspacher," the captain growled, "I'd like to lock up the ship, so if you wouldn't mind turning in—"

Miss Anspacher pouted. "You've interrupted such an interesting conversation. And I don't see why you have to lock up the ship. After all, the night is three hundred and eighty-five hours long. We don't sleep all that time and it would be a shame to be cooped up."

"I'm going to try to rig up some floodlights," Greenfield explained stiffly, "so we won't be caught like this again. Nobody bothered to tell me the day equals thirty-two of ours, so that half of it would be night."

"Then I won't see you for almost two weeks of our time, Jrann-Pttt? Are you sure you wouldn't like to spend the rest of the night in our ship? Plenty of room, you know."

"No, thank you, dear lady. The jungle is my natural habitat. I should feel stultified by walls and a ceiling. Don't worry—I shan't run away."

"Oh, I'm not worried," Miss Anspacher said coyly, throwing a stick of wood on the fire.

"Small riddance if he does."

"Captain Greenfield!"

That part of the captain's face not concealed by his piratical black beard turned red. "Well, if he can read our minds, he knows damn well what I'm thinking, anyway, so why be hypocritical about it?"

"That's right—he is a telepath, isn't he?" Miss Anspacher's face grew even redder than the captain's. "I forgot he. . . . It *is* getting late. I really must go. Good night, Jrann-Pttt."

"Good night, dear lady." The saurian bowed low over her hand.

Leaning on the captain's brawny arm, Miss Anspacher ploughed through the mud to the ship, followed by the mosquito-bat and Algol, who had been toasting themselves more or less companionably at the fire. The door to the airlock clanged behind all four of them.

*

The other saurian's head appeared again from the bush. *Jrann-Pttt, the insistent thought came, shall I rescue you now?*

COLLECTOR'S ITEM

Why, Dfar-Lll? I am not a prisoner. I'm quite free to come and go as I please. But let's get away from the strangers' ship while we communicate. They do have a certain amount of low-grade perception and might be able to sense the presence of another personality. At any rate, they might look out of a port and see you.

Keeping the illuminator on low beam, Dfar-Lll led the way through the bushes. *Seems to me you're going to an awful lot of trouble just to get zoo specimens,* the youngster protested, disentangling its arms from the embrace of an amorous vine. *There's really no reason for carrying on the work since Lieutenant Merglyt-Ruuu . . . passed on.*

Jrann-Pttt sat down on a fallen log and, tucking up his graceful tail, signaled his junior to join him. *In the event that we do decide to return to base, some handsome specimens might serve to offset the lieutenant's demise.*

Return to base? But I thought we were. . . .

We haven't found swamp life pleasant, have we? After all, there's no real reason why we shouldn't go back. Is it our fault that Merglyt-Ruuu happened to meet with a fatal accident?

We-ell . . . but will the commandant see it that way?

On the other hand, if we don't go back, wouldn't it be a good idea to attach ourselves to an expedition that, no matter how alien, is better equipped for survival than we? And carrying out our original purpose seemed the best way of getting to meet these strangers informally, as it were.

They are unquestionably intelligent life-forms then?

After a fashion. Jrann-Pttt yawned and rose. *But why are we sitting here? Let's start back to our camp. We will be able to converse more comfortably.*

They made their way through the jungle—now walking, now wading where the mud became water. Small creatures with hardly any thoughts scurried before them as they went.

14

The commandant may have already made contact with their rulers, Dfar-Lll suggested, springing forward to illuminate the way. *In that case, we couldn't hope to remain undiscovered for long.*

Oh, these creatures are not Venusians. There's no intelligent life here. They hail from the third planet of this system and, according to their thoughts, this is the only vessel that was capable of traversing interplanetary space. So we needn't worry about extradition treaties or any other official annoyances.

If they're friendly, why didn't you spend the night in their ship? It certainly looks more comfortable than our collapsible moslak—which, by the way, collapsed while you were gone. I hope we'll be able to put it up again ourselves. I must say this for the lieutenant—he was good at that sort of thing.

Jrann-Pttt made a gesture of distaste. *He was unfortunately good at other things, too. But let's not discuss him. I'm not staying with the strangers because I want to pick up one or two little things—mostly some of our food to serve them. I used up all the supplies in my pack and I want them to think we're living off the land. They believe me to be a primitive and it's best that they should until I decide just how I'm going to make most efficient use of them. Besides, I didn't want to leave you alone.*

The younger saurian sniffed skeptically.

*

"Honestly, Pitt," Mrs. Bernardi said, keeping to leeward of the tablecloth the lizard-man was efficiently shaking out of the airlock, "I've never had a—an employee as competent as you." But the word she had in mind, of course, was "servant." "I do wish you'd come back to Earth with us."

"Perhaps you would compel me to come?" he suggested, as Algol and the mosquito-bat entered into hot competition to catch the crumbs before they sank into the purple ooze.

"Oh, no! We'd want you to come as our guest—our friend." *Naturally,* her thoughts ran, *a house guest would be expected to help with the washing up and lend a hand with the cooking—and, of course, we wouldn't have to pay him. Though my husband, I suppose, would requisition him as a specimen.*

I fully intend to go to Earth with them, Jrann-Pttt mused, but certainly not in that capacity. Nor would I care to be a specimen. I must formulate some concrete plan.

The captain was crawling on top of the spaceship, scraping off the dried mud, brushing away the leaves and dust that marred its shining purity. The hot, humid haze that poured down from the yellow clouds made the metal surface a little hell. Yet it was hardly less warm on the other side of the clearing, where Miss Anspacher tried desperately to write up her notes on a table that kept sinking into the spongy ground, and hindered by the thick wind that had arisen half an hour before and which kept blowing her papers off. The sweet odor of the flowers tucked in the open neck of her already grimy white blouse suddenly sickened her and she flung them into the mud.

"We won't be going back to Earth for a long time!" she called. Gathering up the purple-stained papers, she came toward the others, little puffs of mist rising at each step. "We like it here. Lovely country."

How could she think to please even the savage she fancied him to be by such an inanity, Jrann-Pttt wondered. No one could possibly like that fetid swamp. Or was it not so much that she was trying to please him as convince herself? Was there some reason the terrestrials had for needing to like Venus. It hovered on the edge of the women's minds. If only it would emerge completely, he could pick it up, but it lurked in the shadows of their subconscious, tantalizing him.

"I'd like to know when we're going to start putting up the shelters," Mrs. Bernardi said, pushing a streak of fog-yellow hair out of her eyes. "I can't stand being cooped up for another night on that ship."

"You're planning to put up shelters—to live outside of the ship?" This would seem to confirm his darkest suspicions. Even a temporary settlement would leave them too open to visitation from the commandant. What his attitude toward the aliens might be, Jrann-Pttt didn't know. He might consider them as specimens, as enemies or as potential allies. What his attitude toward Jrann-Pttt and his companion would be, however, the saurian knew only too well. Had they reported the lieutenant's demise immediately, it was possible the commandant might have been brought to believe it was an accident. Now he would unquestionably think Jrann-Pttt had killed Merglyt-Ruuu on purpose—which was not true; how was Jrann-Pttt to know that the mud into which he'd knocked the lieutenant was quicksand?

"Anything against putting up shelters?" Captain Greenfield growled from his perch.

"Monster!" the mosquito-bat shrieked at the cat. "Monster! Monster!"

*

There was a painfully embarrassed silence.

"The creature is not intelligent," Jrann-Pttt explained, smiling. "It merely has vocal apparatus that can reproduce a frequently heard word, like—you have a bird, I believe, a—" he searched their minds for the word—"a parrot."

"Monster!" the mosquito-bat continued. "Monster! Monster!"

"Shut up or I'll wring your neck!" the captain snarled. The mosquito-bat obeyed sullenly, apparently recognizing the threat in his tone.

COLLECTOR'S ITEM

But the concept of "monster" hung heavily in the air between the terrestrials and the lizard-man. *They should not feel so bad about it,* he thought, *for they are the monsters themselves. But that would never occur to them and I can hardly reassure them by saying. . . .*

"Don't worry," Professor Bernardi said smoothly. "To him, it's we who are the monsters."

A sudden gust of wind nearly whipped the tablecloth out of Jrann-Pttt's hands. He fought with it for a moment, glad of something tangible to contend with. "About the shelters," he said. "They might not stand up against a storm."

"So this is monsoon country," Bernardi observed thoughtfully. "Do you know when the storms usually come, Jrann-Pttt?" The other shook his head. "Peculiar. There usually is a season for that sort of thing."

"I . . . come from another part of the planet."

"Storms here are bad, eh?" the captain commented, swinging himself down easily. "Frankly, that worries me. Ship's resting on mud as far as I can see, and if there's one thing I do know something about, it's mud. If it got any wetter, the ship might sink."

"Maybe we should leave," Mrs. Bernardi suggested. "Go to another part of the planet where it's drier, or—" she tried not to show the sudden surge of hope—"leave for home and come back after the rainy season."

There was a sudden silence, and Jrann-Pttt found himself able to pick up the answers to some of his questions from the alien minds. His worst fears were confirmed. Plan A was out. But something could still be done with these creatures.

"Doesn't she know?" the captain demanded accusingly. "You brought her here without telling her?"

Bernardi spread his hands wide in a futile gesture. "She should know; I've told her repeatedly. She just doesn't understand . . . or doesn't want to."

"I know they'll forgive us," Mrs. Bernardi said stubbornly. "We—you—haven't done anything really wrong, so how could they do anything terrible to us? After all, didn't they refuse you the funds because they said you couldn't—"

"Shhh, Louisa," her husband commanded.

Jrann-Pttt smiled to himself.

—"do it," she went on. "And you did. So they were wrong and they'll have to forgive us."

"Tcha!" Miss Anspacher said. "Since when was there any fairness in justice?"

"On the other hand," Mrs. Bernardi continued, "we have no idea of how dangerous the storms here could be."

"Very dangerous," Jrann-Pttt said.

"For you, perhaps," the captain retorted. "Maybe not for us."

"Now that's silly," Miss Anspacher said. "You can see that Jrann-Pttt is much more—" she blushed—"sturdily built than we are."

"I don't mean that we could face it without protection," the captain replied angrily. "Naturally I mean that our superior technology could cope with the effects of any storm."

"Well, Captain, we'll have to put that superior technology to use at once," the professor told him. "You'd better start blasting that rock."

Laden with equipment and malevolent thoughts, the captain trudged off into the murky jungle. The others would not even offer to help. Confounded scientists; they certainly took his status as captain seriously. He wished, for a disloyal moment, that he had stayed on Earth. The quiet routine of a test pilot had prepared him for nothing like this. Were Miss Anspacher and adventure worth it?

19

COLLECTOR'S ITEM

At the moment, he thought not. But he was on Venus and it was too late to change his mind.

Jrann-Pttt followed him into the jungle, keeping some distance behind, for he had good reason to suspect that Greenfield would take his warm interest in terrestrial technology for plain spying. Or, worse yet, he might try to press the lizard-man into service; Jrann-Pttt felt he had demeaned himself quite enough already.

"Have you noticed," Miss Anspacher asked, pushing the mass of damp brown hair off her neck as she came alongside him, "how the—the smell—" *a scientist does not mince words*—"of the swamp has grown stronger?"

Jrann-Pttt halted. He had a good idea of what the captain's reactions to the sight of himself and Miss Anspacher arriving hand-in-hand would be. "Yes, it is getting rather overpowering. Perhaps, for a lady of your delicate sensibilities, it would be best to—"

"I can stand a bad smell just as well as a male—any male!"

"Perhaps even better," Jrann-Pttt said, "for I was on the verge of turning back myself."

"Oh," she said, appeased. "Well, in that case, I'll go back with you . . . how quiet everything is!"

He had not noticed. For him, it would never be quiet because of the stream of jangled thoughts constantly pouring into the back of his mind from everything sentient that surrounded him.

For a moment, he wondered what it would be like to be non-telepathic like the terrestrials, to have peace from the clamor of confused impressions, emotions and ideas that persistently beat at his mind. But that would be wondering how it was to be deaf to avoid discord, or blind to shut out ugliness.

"The lull before the storm, I suppose," she said brightly. *Now is his opportunity to kiss me—only perhaps they don't have kissing in his society. His*

20

mouth does seem to be the wrong shape. And if I kissed him, it might violate a taboo.

During their short absence, the citrine clouds that closed off the sky had changed to a sinister umber. It was now almost as dusky in the clearing as in the jungle itself, when Jrann-Pttt and Miss Anspacher returned and joined the others.

Professor Bernardi stood looking up with sharp gray eyes at a sky he could not see. "I hope Greenfield can finish the blasting more quickly than he estimated," he muttered.

"Will we hear the noise way out here, Carl?" his wife worried nervously.

"Only two kilometers away? Of course we'll hear it. I do wish you wouldn't always be asking such stupid questions."

She shivered. "Well, I hope they get it over with right away. If we just have to sit here waiting and waiting and waiting, I'll go mad. I know I will."

"You should try to keep your nerves in check, Louisa," Miss Anspacher snapped. *Silly little fool.*

"At least I can control my glands!" Mrs. Bernardi flared back. *Sex-starved spinster.*

"I shall make some tea, ladies," Jrann-Pttt interposed. "I'm sure we will all feel the better for it."

Mrs. Bernardi smiled at him feebly. "You're such a comfort, Pitt. I don't know why you of all creatures should be the one to remind me of home."

"Home," remarked Mortland, emerging from the airlock, "is where the heart is. Did I hear someone say 'tea'?"

*

As Jrann-Pttt hung the kettle over the fire, suddenly the air erupted in stunning violence of sound. The ground undulated under their

21

feet and water slopped out of the kettle, almost putting out the fire that rose high to claw at it. Rivulets of thick, muddy liquid welled out of the ground and drabbled their feet. The women turned pale. Algol gave a faint cry and hid under Mrs. Bernardi's skirts, trembling, while the mosquito-bat tried to lift Mortland's toupee and hide in his hair. The ship itself quivered and seemed to jump slightly in the air, then returned to its resting place.

All was quiet again, quieter than it had been before. Mortland anxiously gnawed his light mustache. "Better hurry with that tea, there's a good fellow. I'm violently allergic to loud noises."

"They'll probably continue all day," the professor said with almost malevolent cheerfulness, "so you might as well get used to them." *Who is he to have nerves? I am easily the most sensitive person here, but I manage to control myself.*

"I don't know how I'm going to stand it!" Mrs. Bernardi shrieked. "I just know something terrible is going to happen."

"Please try to restrain yourself, Louisa," her husband ordered. "After it's over, you'll find we'll be much more comfortable and secure with the ship resting on rock."

"If you ask me, that blast made it sink a little," Mortland said. "I wonder whether—"

He was interrupted by a thrashing in the bushes. Dfar-Lll burst forth, shedding scales. *Do not despair, Jrann-Pttt. I am here, ready to save you or die at your side.*

The women clutched each other, Miss Anspacher praying silently and fervently to Juno, Lakshmi, Freya, Isis and a host of other esoteric female deities she had picked up in the course of her avocational researches.

"He seems to be one of Jrann-Pttt's people," Bernardi observed, "so there should be nothing to fear."

Dfar-Lll, you fool! Jrann-Pttt ideated angrily. *Nothing's wrong. They're just blasting out a better berth for their vessel. And now you've spoiled my plans.*

"What did you think at that poor little creature!" Mrs. Bernardi blazed. "He's crying!" And, sure enough, amethyst tears were oozing out of the young saurian's large, liquid eyes.

I du-didn't mean any harm.

"Monster!" Mrs. Bernardi accused Jrann-Pttt. "All men are monsters, whether they're aliens or not."

"You're so right, Louisa!" Miss Anspacher exclaimed, regarding the younger creature in an almost kindly manner.

I'm sorry, r-Lll, Jrann-Pttt apologized. *I was upset by that noise, too. How could you possibly know what it was? Come, let me introduce you to the creatures.*

Dfar-Lll stepped forward diffidently. Jrann-Pttt put a hand on the moss-green shoulder. "Allow me to introduce my companion, Dfar-Lll," he said aloud.

The youngster looked at him.

Mrs. Bernardi thrust out her hand. "I'm very glad to meet you, Lil."

Agitate it with one of yours. It's a courtesy. Don't let her see how repulsive she is to you. Remember, you're just as repulsive to her.

Dfar-Lll offered a shy, seven-fingered hand. "Pleased . . . to meet you . . . ma'am," the young lizard squeaked.

"Why, he's just a baby, isn't he?" Mrs. Bernardi asked.

I am not a baby! Dfar-Lll thought indignantly. *At the end of this year, I shall celebrate my pre-maturity feast, or I would have. And furthermore—*

There was another thunderous blast of sound. After the ground had stopped trembling, the six found themselves ankle-deep in muddy water. Algol, who was in considerably deeper than his ankles, mewed fretfully. Mrs. Bernardi picked him up and comforted him.

23

COLLECTOR'S ITEM

"Perhaps blasting wasn't such a good idea," the professor muttered. "Maybe I should tell Greenfield to call a halt and we'll take our chances with the storm. As a matter of fa—"

"The ship!" Mortland cried. "It *is* sinking!"

And the big metal ball slowly but visibly was indeed subsiding into the mud.

"Stop it, somebody!" Miss Anspacher snapped in her customary schoolroom manner.

The professor was pale, but he held on to his calm. "What can we do? Even if we could get the captain back in time, there's no way we can stop it. It's too heavy to pull out manually, and the engines, of course, are inside."

As they watched in horror, the ship sank deeper and deeper, picking up momentum as more of it went under. With a loud, sucking sound, it vanished into the ooze. Muddy water gurgled over it and, where the ship had been, there was now a small lake.

"This could be the beginning of a legend," Miss Anspacher murmured. "Or the end."

There was another vibrant detonation. "Someone ought to go tell the captain there's no use blasting any more," Bernardi said wearily. "We have nothing to put on the rock when he smooths it off." He began to laugh. "I suppose you could call this poetic justice." And he went on laughing, losing a bit of his former self-control.

There goes Plan B, Jrann-Pttt thought.

A star of intensely bright green lightning split the clouds and widened to cover the visible expanse of sky. There was a planet-shaking clap of thunder that made Greenfield's puny efforts sound like the snapping of twigs in comparison and it began to rain hard and fast.

*

"If only I hadn't gone and blasted that damn rock," the captain grumbled, squeezing water out of his shirt-tails, "we'd have been all right. Probably the storm wouldn't have done a thing to the ship except get it wet. If you can even call it a storm."

"I can and I do," Jrann-Pttt replied, haughtily squeegeeing his wet scales. "All I said was that a storm might be coming up and it might be dangerous. How was I to know it would last only half an hour?"

"Even the camp stools pulled through," Greenfield pointed out, "and you said shelters wouldn't stand up."

"I only said they might not. Can't you understand your own language?"

The fissure in the clouds had not quite closed yet and through it the enormous, blazing disk of the sun glared at them, twice as large as it appeared from Earth. It was a moot point as to whether they'd be dried out or steamed alive first.

"Might as well collect whatever gear we have left and get it to higher ground," Miss Anspacher said efficiently. "Two feet of water won't do anything any good—even those camp stools."

"It's my belief you wanted this to happen," Greenfield accused Jrann-Pttt. "You wanted to get rid of us."

"My dear fellow," Jrann-Pttt replied loftily, "the information I gave you was, to the best of my knowledge, accurate. However, I happen to be a professor of zoology and not a meteorologist. Apparently you people live out in the open like primitives," he continued, ignoring Dfar-Lll's admiring interjection, "and are accustomed to the vicissitudes of weather. I am a civilized creature; I live—" *or used to live*—"in an air-conditioned, light-conditioned, weather-conditioned city. It is only when I rough it on field trips like this to trackless parts of the—globe that I am forced to experience weather. Even then, I have never before been caught in a situation like this."

COLLECTOR'S ITEM

In fact, I was never before caught or I wouldn't be in this situation at all.

"Oh, Jrann-Pttt," sighed Miss Anspacher, "I knew you couldn't be just an ordinary native!"

"How did you get into this situation then?" Professor Bernardi asked. He had an unfortunate talent for going directly to the point.

"The third member of our expedition died," Jrann-Pttt explained. "He was our dirigational expert. Our guide."

"How did he happen to—"

"Are we just going to stand here chatting," Miss Anspacher demanded, "or are we going to do something about this?"

"What can we do?" Mrs. Bernardi asked weakly. "We might just as well lie down and—"

"Never say die, Louisa," Miss Anspacher admonished.

"I suggest we go to my camp to see what shape it's in," Jrann-Pttt said, furiously putting together Plan C. "Some of the supplies there might prove useful."

Captain Greenfield looked questioningly at Bernardi. The professor shrugged. "Might as well."

"All right," the captain growled. "Let's pick up whatever we can save."

*

Since there wasn't much that could be rescued, the little safari was soon on its way. Jrann-Pttt led, carrying Algol in his arms. Behind came Mortland, bearing a camp stool and the kettle into which he had tucked a tin of biscuits and into which the mosquito-bat had tucked itself, its orange eyes glaring out angrily from beneath the lid. Next came Mrs. Bernardi with her knitting, her camp stool and her sorrow.

Dfar-Lll followed with two stools and the plastic tea set. Close behind was Miss Anspacher, with the sugar bowl, the earthenware teapot and an immense bound volume of the *Proceedings of the Physical Society of Ameranglis* for 1993. Professor Bernardi bore a briefcase full of notes and the table. The rain had damaged the latter's mechanism, so that its legs kept unfolding from time to time, to the great inconvenience of Captain Greenfield, who brought up the rear with the blasting equipment. Behind them and sometimes alongside them came something—or someone—else.

"Surely your camp must have been closer to ours than this," Miss Anspacher finally remarked after they had been slogging through mud and water and pushing aside reluctant vegetation for over an Earth hour.

"I am very much afraid," Jrann-Pttt admitted, "that our camp has been lost—that is to say, inundated."

"What are we going to do now?" the captain asked of the company at large.

Professor Bernardi shrugged. "Our only course would seem to be making for one of the cities and throwing ourselves upon the na—Jrann-Pttt's people's hospitality. If Professor Jrann-Pttt has even the vaguest idea of the direction in which his home lies, we might as well head that way." *I wonder whether the natives could help us raise the ship.*

"I'm sure my people will be more than happy to welcome you," Jrann-Pttt said smoothly, "and to make you comfortable until your people send another ship to fetch you."

The terrestrials looked at one another. Dfar-Lll looked at Jrann-Pttt.

Professor Bernardi coughed. "That was the only spaceship we had," he admitted. "The first experimental model, you know." *We don't expect to stay on this awful planet forever. After all, as Louisa says, the government will have to forgive us. Public opinion and all that.*

"Oh," the saurian said. "Then we shall have the pleasure of your company until they build another?"

There was silence. "We have the only plans," the professor said, gripping his briefcase more tightly. "I am the inventor of the ship, so naturally I would have them." *If we brought back some specimens of Venusian life—of intelligent Venusian life—to prove we'd been here. . . .*

"Matter of fact, old fellow," Mortland said, "we took all the plans with us so they couldn't build another ship and follow—"

"Mortland!" the professor exclaimed.

"But they're telepaths," Miss Anspacher said. "They must know already."

Everyone turned to look at the saurians.

"I have . . . certain information," Jrann-Pttt admitted, "but I cannot understand it. You are in trouble with your rulers because they would not give you the funds, claiming space travel was impossible?"

"That's right," Bernardi said. *Not really specimens, you understand. Guests.*

"And you went ahead and appropriated the funds and materials from your government, since you were in a trusted position where you could do so?"

Bernardi nodded.

"Of course the question is now academic, for the ship is gone, but since you proved the possibility of space travel by coming here, wouldn't your government then dismiss the charges against you?"

"That's exactly what I keep telling him!" Mrs. Bernardi exclaimed.

But her husband shook his head. "The law is inflexible. We have broken it and must be punished, even if by breaking it we proved its fundamental error." *Why let him know our plans?*

Why, Jrann-Pttt, that sounds just like our own government, doesn't it?

Yes, it does. We should be able to establish a very satisfactory mode of living with these strangers.

"We'd hoped that after a year or so the whole thing would die down," Mortland explained frankly, "and we'd go back as heroes."

"Do you know the way to your home, Jrann-Pttt?" the professor asked anxiously.

"Since we were able to catch a glimpse of the sun, I think I can figure out roughly where we are. All we must do is walk some two hundred kilometers in that direction—" he waved an arm to indicate the way—"and we should be at the capital."

"Will your people accept us as refugees?" Miss Anspacher demanded bluntly, "or will we be captives?" *Which is what I'll bet the good professor is planning for you, if only he can figure some way to get you and, of course, ourselves back.*

"We should be proud to accept you as citizens and to receive the benefits of your splendid technology. Our laboratories will be placed at your disposal."

"Well, that's better than we hoped for," the professor said, brightening. "We had expected to have to carve our own laboratories out of the wilderness. Now we shall be able to carry on our researches in comfort." *No need to trouble the natives; we'll be able to raise the ship ourselves. Or build a new one. And I'll see to it personally that they have special quarters in the zoo with a considerable amount of privacy.*

"If I were you, I wouldn't trust him too far," the captain warned. "He's a foreigner."

"You ought to be ashamed of yourself, Captain!" Miss Anspacher said. "I, for one, trust Jrann-Pttt implicitly. Did you say this direction, Jrann-Pttt?" She stepped forward briskly. There was a loud splash and water closed over her head.

COLLECTOR'S ITEM

Captain Greenfield rushed forward to haul her out. "Well," she said, daintily coughing up mud, "I was wet to begin with, anyway."

"You're a brave little woman, Miss Anspacher," the captain told her admiringly.

"This sort of thing may present a problem," Professor Bernardi commented. "I hope that was only a pot-hole, that the water is not going to be consistently too deep for wading."

"There might be quicksand, too," Mrs. Bernardi said somberly. "In quicksand, one drowns slowly."

Dfar-Lll gave a start. *Surely you don't intend to lead them back to base?*

Precisely. The swamp is unfit for settlement.

But to return voluntarily to captivity?

Who mentioned anything about captivity? Assisted by our new friends, we have an excellent chance of taking over the ship and supplies by a surprise attack.

But why should these aliens assist us?

Jrann-Pttt smiled. *Oh, I think they will. Yes, I have every confidence in Plan C.*

"I suggest," the professor said, ignoring his wife's pessimism, "that each one of us pull a branch from a tree. We can test the ground before we step on it, to make sure that there is solid footing underneath."

"Good idea," the captain approved. He reached out the arm that was not occupied with Miss Anspacher and tugged at a tree limb.

And then he and the lady physicist were both floundering in the ooze.

"Well, really, Captain Greenfield!" she cried, refusing his aid in extricating herself. "I always thought you were at least a gentleman in spite of your illiteracy!"

"Wha—what happened?" he asked as he struggled out of the mud. "Something pushed me; I swear it."

Jrann-Pttt mentalized. "It seems the tree did not like your trying to remove a branch."

"The tree!" Greenfield's pale blue eyes bulged. "You're joking!"

"Not at all. As a matter of fact, I myself have been wondering why there were so many thought-streams and yet so few animals around here. It never occurred to me that the vegetation could be sentient and have such strong emotive defenses. In all my experience as a botanist, I—"

"I thought you were a zoologist," Bernardi interrupted.

"My people do not believe in excessive specialization," the saurian replied.

"Trees that think?" Mortland inquired incredulously.

"They're not very bright," Jrann-Pttt explained, "but they don't like having their limbs pulled off. I don't suppose you would, either, for that matter."

"I propose," Miss Anspacher said, shaking out her wet hair, "that we break up the camp stools and use the sticks instead of branches to help us along."

"Good idea," the captain said, trying to get back into her good graces. "I always knew women could put their brains to use if they tried."

She glared at him.

"I thought we'd use the furniture to make a fire later," Mortland complained. "For tea, you know."

"The ground's much too wet," Professor Bernardi replied.

"And besides," Miss Anspacher added, "I lost the teapot in that pot-hole."

COLLECTOR'S ITEM

"But you managed to save the *Proceedings of the Physical Society*," Mortland snarled. "Serve you right if I eat it. And I warn you, if hard-pressed, I shall."

"How will we cook our food, though?" Mrs. Bernardi demanded apprehensively. "It's a lucky thing, Mr. Pitt, that we have you with us to tell us which of the berries and things are edible, so at least we shan't starve."

The visible portion of Jrann-Pttt's well-knit form turned deeper green. "But I regret to say I don't know, Mrs. Bernardi. Those 'native' foods I served you were all synthetics from our personal stores. I never tasted natural foods before I met you."

"And if the trees don't like our taking their branches," Miss Anspacher put in, "I don't suppose the bushes would like our taking their berries. Louisa, don't do that!"

But Mrs. Bernardi, with her usual disregard for orders, had fainted into the mud. Pulling her out and reviving her caused so much confusion, it wasn't until then that they discovered Algol had disappeared.

*

The party had been trudging through mud and water and struggling with pale, malevolent vines and bushes and low-hanging branches for close to six Earth hours. All of them were tired and hungry, now that their meager supply of biscuits and chocolate was gone.

"Remember, Carl," Mrs. Bernardi told her husband, "I forgive you. And I know I'm being foolishly sentimental, but if you could manage to take my body back to Earth—"

"Don't be so pessimistic." Professor Bernardi absent-mindedly leaned against a tree, then recoiled as he remembered it might resent

32

being treated like an inanimate object. "In any case, we'll most likely all die at the same time."

"I never did want to go to Venus, really," Mrs. Bernardi sniffled. "I only came, like Algol did, because I didn't have any choice. If you left me behind, I'd have had to bear the brunt of. . . . Where is Algol?" She stared at Jrann-Pttt. "You were carrying him. What have you done with him?"

The lizard-man looked at her in consternation. "He jumped out of my arms when you fainted and I turned back to help. I was certain one of the others had him."

"He's dead!" she wailed. "You let him fall into the water and drown—an innocent kitty that never hurt anybody, except in fun."

"Come, come, Louisa." Her husband took her arm. "He was only a cat. I'm sure Jrann-Pttt didn't mean for him to drown. He was just so upset by your fainting that he didn't think. . . . "

"Not Jrann-Pttt's fault, of course," Miss Anspacher said.

"After all, we can't expect them to love animals as we do. But Algol was a very good sort of cat. . . . "

"Keep quiet, all of you!" Jrann-Pttt shouted. "I have never known any species to use any method of communication so much in order to communicate so little. Don't you understand? I would not have assumed the cat was with one of you, if I had not subconsciously sensed his thought-stream all along. He must be nearby."

Everyone was still, while Jrann-Pttt probed the dense underbrush that blocked their view on both sides. "Over here," he announced, and led the way through the thick screen of interlaced bushes and vines on the left.

About ten meters farther on, the ground sloped up sharply to form a ridge rising a meter and a half above the rest of the terrain. The water had not reached its blunted top, and on this fairly level strip of ground, perhaps three meters wide, Algol had been paralleling their path in dry-pawed comfort.

"Scientists!" Louisa Bernardi almost spat. "Professors! We could have been walking on that, too. But did anybody think to look for dry ground? No! It was wet in one place, so it would be wet in another. Oh, Algol—" she reached over to embrace the cat—"you're smarter than any so-called intelligent life-forms."

He indignantly straightened a whisker she had crumpled.

*

"Look," Mortland exclaimed in delight as they attained the top of the ridge, "here are some dryish twigs! Don't suppose the trees want them, since they've let them fall. If I can get a fire going, we could boil some swamp water and make tea. Nasty thought, but it's better than no tea at all. And how long can one go on living without tea?"

"We'll need some food before long, too," Professor Bernardi observed, putting his briefcase down on a fallen log. "The usual procedure, I believe, would be for us to draw straws to see which gets eaten—although there isn't any hurry."

"I'm glad then that we'll be able to have a fire," Mortland said, busily collecting twigs. "I should hate to have to eat you raw, Carl."

Mr. Pitt and his little friend are delightful creatures, Mrs. Bernardi thought. *So intelligent and so well behaved. But eating them wouldn't really be cannibalism. They aren't people.*

That premise works both ways, dear lady, Jrann-Pttt ideated. *And I must say your species will prove far easier to peel for the cooking pot.*

"Monster! What are you doing?" Mortland dropped his twigs and pulled the mosquito-bat away from a bush. "Don't eat those berries, you silly ass; the bush won't like it!" The mosquito-bat piped wrathfully.

Jrann-Pttt probed with intentness. "You know, I rather think the bush wants its berries to be eaten. Something to do with—er—propagating itself. Of course it has a false impression as to what is going to be done with the berries, but the important fact is that it won't put up any resistance."

"All right, old fellow." Mortland released the mosquito-bat, which promptly flew back to the bush. "I'm not the custodian of your morals."

"I wonder whether we could eat those berries, too," Professor Bernardi remarked pensively.

"Carl!" Mrs. Bernardi's tear-stained face flushed pink. "Why—why, that's almost indecent!"

"We eat beans, don't we?" Mortland pointed out. "They're seeds."

"We also eat meat," Miss Anspacher added.

There was silence. "I imagine," Mrs. Bernardi murmured, "it's because we never get to meet the meat socially." She avoided the saurians' eyes.

"We'd better see how Monster makes out, though," Miss Anspacher observed, replenishing her lipstick, "before we try the berries ourselves. The fact that the bush is anxious to dispose of them doesn't mean they can't be poisonous."

"Why should Monster sacrifice himself for us?" Mortland retorted hotly, overlooking the fact that Monster's purpose in eating the berries was almost certainly not an altruistic one. "If we can risk his life, we can risk our own." He crammed a handful of berries into his mouth defiantly. "I say, they're good!"

Algol sniffed the bush with disgust, then turned away.

"See?" said Miss Anspacher. "They're undoubtedly poisonous. When he's really hungry, he isn't so fussy." She combed her hair.

"But is he really hungry?" Bernardi asked suspiciously. "Come here, Algol. Nice kitty." He bent down and sniffed the cat's breath. The cat sniffed his interestedly. Their whiskers touched. "I thought so. Fish!"

"You mean," Mrs. Bernardi shrieked, "that while we were struggling through that water, alternately starving and drowning by centimeters, that wretched cat has not only been walking along here dry as toast, but gorging himself on fish?"

"Now, now, Mrs. Bernardi," Jrann-Pttt said. "Being a dumb animal, he wouldn't think of informing you about matters of which he'd assume that you, as the superior beings, would be fully cognizant."

"You might have told us there were fish on this planet, Mr. Pitt."

"Dear lady, there is something I feel I should tell you. I am not—"

"They're here on the other side of the ridge," Greenfield called, bending over and peering through the foliage. "The fish, I mean."

"The pools look shallow," Bernardi said, also bending over. "The fish should be easy enough to catch. Might even be able to get them in our hands." He reached out to demonstrate, proving the error of both his theses, for the fish slipped right through his fingers and, as he grabbed for them, he lost his balance, toppled over the side of the ridge into the mud and water below and began to disappear, showing beyond a doubt that the pools were deeper than he had thought.

"Carl, what are you doing?" Mrs. Bernardi peered into the murky depths where her husband was threshing about. "Why don't you come out of that filthy mud?"

His voice, though muffled, was still acid. "It isn't mud, my dear. It's quicksand!"

"Rope!" the captain exclaimed, grabbing a coil.

"Hold on, chaps!" cried a squeaky voice. "I'm coming to the rescue!" A stout twelve-foot vine plunged out of the shadows and wrapped one end of itself around a tree—disregarding the latter's violent objections—and the other end around Professor Bernardi's thorax, which was just disappearing into the mud. "Now if one or two of you would haul away, we'll soon have him out all shipshape and proper. Heave ho! Don't be afraid of hurting me; my strength is as the strength of ten because my heart is pure."

"It's that vine!" Dfar-Lll exclaimed. "So that's what has been following us all along!"

*

"I can accept the idea of a vegetable thinking," Professor Bernardi gasped as he was pulled out of the quicksand, "although with the utmost reluctance." He shook himself like a dog. "But how can it be mobile?"

"You chaps can move around," the vine explained, "so I said to myself: 'Dammit, I'll have a shot at doing that, too.' Hard going at first, when you're using suckers, but I persevered and I made it. Look, I can talk, too. Never heard of a vine doing that before, did you? Fact is, I hadn't thought of it before, but then I never had anyone to communicate with. All those other vines are so stupid; you have absolutely no idea! Hope you don't mind my picking up your language, but it was the only one around—"

"We are honored," Professor Bernardi declared. "And I am deeply grateful to you, too, sir or madam, for saving my life."

"Think nothing of it," the vine said, arranging its leaves, which were of a pleasing celadon rather than the whitish-green favored by the rest of the local vegetation. "Now that I can move, I'll probably be doing heroic things like that all the time. Are you all going to the city? May I go with you? I've heard lots about the city," it went on, taking consent for granted, "but I never thought I'd get to see it. Everybody in the swamp is such an old stick-in-the-mud. I thought I was trapped, too, forced to spend the rest of my life in a provincial environment. Is it true that the streets are filled with chlorophyll? Do you think I can get a job in a botanical garden or something? Perhaps I can give little talks on horticulture to visitors?"

The mosquito-bat looked out of the tea kettle austerely. "Monster!" it piped shrilly.

"The very idea!" the vine snapped back indignantly. "Oh, well," it said, calming down, "you probably don't know any better. It's up to me as the intelligent life-form to forgive you, and I shall."

Jrann-Pttt and Dfar-Lll looked at each other in consternation. *Do you think there really are cities on this planet, sir? Can there be indigenous intelligent life? If so, it may have already got in touch with the commandant.*

Impossible, Jrann-Pttt replied. *The vine probably just heard us talking about a city. After all, it picked up the language that way; very likely it absorbed some terrestrial concepts along with it. If there are any real settlements at all, they must be quite primitive—nothing more than villages. No, it's we who will build the cities on Venus. Combining our technology with the terrestrials', we could develop a pretty little civilization here—after we've disposed of the commandant, so he can't report our disappearance. We don't want any publicity. So much better to keep our little society exclusive.*

*

"Wonder what time it is," the captain remarked as he rose and stretched in the dim yellow light of the long Venusian day. "Must have slept for hours. My watch seems to have stopped."

"Mine, too." Mortland unstrapped his from his wrist and shook it futilely. "Waterproof, hah! If we ever get back to Earth, I shall make the manufacturer eat his guarantee."

"Oh, well, what does time matter to us now?" Professor Bernardi pointed out as he rose from his leafy couch with a loud creak. All of them—even the saurians—had aches and pains in every joint and muscle as a result of the unaccustomed exercise and the damp climate. "We are out of its reach. It has no present meaning for us."

This depressed them all. Only the vine seemed in good health and spirits. "I notice you're all wearing clothes except for the short four-legged gentleman with the home-grown fur coat," it chattered happily. "Do you think I'll be socially acceptable without them? I wouldn't want to make a bad impression at the very start—or would leaves do?"

Everybody looked at Jrann-Pttt. "We are not a narrow-minded species," he said hastily. "I'm sure your leaves will be more than adequate."

After a breakfast of fish and berries stewed in tea—which the vine declined with thanks—the various members of the party gathered up their belongings and resumed their journey. Encrusted with dried purple mud and grime, their clothes deliberately torn by anti-social shrubbery, their chins—of the males, that is—disfigured by hirsute growths, the terrestrials made a sorry spectacle. It was hot, boiling hot, and more humid than ever.

"Well," said Miss Anspacher, letting the Swahili marching song with which she had been attempting to encourage the company peter out, "I do hope we'll reach your city soon, Jrann-Pttt. I must say I could use a hot bath." She added hastily, "Hot baths are a peculiar cultural trait of ours."

"I could use one myself," Jrann-Pttt said. He brushed his scales fastidiously.

"I'm looking forward so to meeting your relatives," she said, grabbing his left arm determinedly. "I'm not violating a taboo or anything, am I?" *It isn't really slimy; it just feels that way.*

COLLECTOR'S ITEM

"Not one of my people's. But I'm afraid you are violating a terrestrial taboo, judging from the thoughts I pick up from your captain's mind."

"Oh, him—he's a stupid fool!"

"Not at all. Rough, perhaps. Untutored, yes. But with a good deal of native intelligence, although fearfully primitive."

"Perhaps I was too harsh," Miss Anspacher observed thoughtfully. *The captain . . . is good-looking in a brutal sort of way, although not nearly as handsome or even as spiritual in appearance as Jrann-Pttt. And sometimes I almost think he*—she blushed to herself—*shows a certain partiality for my company.*

She did not, however, let go of the saurian's arm when the captain bustled up, prepared to put a stop to this, but tactfully, if possible, for he had begun to realize that his rude ways did not endear him to her.

"Ah—we're making very good progress, aren't we, Pitt?" he interrupted, trying to insinuate himself between the two.

"Excellent."

"How soon do you think we'll be at your city at this rate?"

Jrann-Pttt shrugged. "Since I have no way of telling what our rate is or how far we have gone, how can I tell? As a matter of fact, you might as well learn now as later—I am not a Venusian. There is no intelligent life native to Venus."

"Oh, really!" the vine interposed indignantly. "Saying a thing like that right in front of me! What would you call me, then, pray tell?"

Jrann-Pttt kept his actual thoughts to himself. "A mutation," he said. "Probably you are the first intelligent life-form to appear upon this planet. Scholarly volumes will be written about you."

"Oh?" The vine seemed to be appeased. "I accept your apology. Perhaps I'll learn to write and do the books myself, because I'm the only one who can understand the real me."

40

"But how can you show us the way to your city if you're not native to Venus?" Bernardi demanded, whirling fretfully upon the saurian. "What is this, anyway? Each time you come up with a different story!"

"See?" said the captain. "Didn't I tell you he was up to no good?"

"I should like to lead you to our base," Jrann-Pttt replied with quiet dignity. "I am telling you the truth now since I feel I should have your consent before proceeding farther."

??????? Dfar-Lll projected.

"I hesitated before, because I wasn't sure I could trust you. You see, the spaceship in which we came to this planet is a prison ship, with a crew consisting of malefactors—thieves, murderers, defrauders—dispatched to the remote fastnesses of the Galaxy to fetch back zoological specimens. Our zoo, I must say, is the finest and most interesting in the Universe."

"Monster!" the mosquito-bat squeaked.

"Shhh," Mortland admonished. "Don't interrupt."

"I was in command of our ill-fated expedition. . . . "

Oh, Dfar-Lll projected. *For a moment there, sir, you had me worried.*

"When we reached Venus, I was, I must admit, careless. I gave the crew a chance to mutiny and they did. Slew most of the officers. Dfar-Lll and I were lucky to escape with our lives."

"But you might have told us!" Mrs. Bernardi's voice held reproach.

"Until we knew what kind of beings you were, we couldn't let you know how helpless and unprotected we were."

The women seemed moved, but not the men.

"Leading us on a wild goose chase, were you?" the captain challenged.

Jrann-Pttt drew a deep breath. "It was my hope that all of you would consent to help us get our ship back from these criminals. Then we could fly to my planet—which is the fifth of the star you know as Alpha Centauri—where, I assure you, you would be hospitably received."

We aren't really going back home, Jrann-Pttt, are we? I'd sooner stay here in the swamp than go back to that jail.

Have confidence in me, r-Lll. As soon as we have disposed of the commandant and his officers, I can put our ship out of commission. The terrestrials won't be able to tell what's wrong. They know nothing about space travel. The fact that they got their crude vessel to operate was probably sheer luck.

But the younger was not to be diverted. *Will we kill them after we've disposed of our officers? I should hate to.*

Certainly not. We shall need servants and I don't trust the prisoners in the ship—all criminals of the lowest type! Aloud, he said to the bewildered terrestrials, "If you don't want to help us, I shall understand. No sense your interfering in another species' quarrels, particularly as we must seem like monsters to you."

"Monster!" the mosquito-bat agreed. "Monster, monster, monster!" No one tried to stop him. Jrann-Pttt sensed that somehow he had lost a good deal of his grip on the terrestrials. Finesse, he thought angrily, was wasted on these barbaric life-forms.

Bernardi sighed. "I suppose we'll have to help you." *No reason why his ship shouldn't stop off at Earth before it goes to Alpha Centauri. No reason why it should even go to Alpha Centauri at all, in fact.*

"If you ask me," the captain said, "he's one of the criminals himself."

"But nobody asked you," Miss Anspacher retorted, the more acidly because she had been wondering the same thing. "Shall we resume our journey?"

"Hold on," the vine said. "I don't want to intrude or anything, but it hasn't been made quite clear to me whether or not I'm included in the invitation to this Alpha Centauri place, and I wouldn't want to keep going only on the off-chance that you might ask me. I really think you should, because you led me astray with your fair promises of glittering cities."

"The cities of our planet do not glitter," Jrann-Pttt replied, wishing it would wither instantly, "but certainly you are invited. Glad to have you."

"Oh, that's awfully decent of you," the vine said emotionally. "I shan't forget it, I promise you."

*

They plodded onward, the vine chattering so incessantly that a faint gurgling which accompanied them went unnoticed. The gurgling grew louder and louder as they pushed on. Finally, "I keep hearing water," Mortland remarked. "We must be approaching a river of some kind."

A few minutes later, bursting through a screen of underbrush, they found themselves confronted by a river whose bubbling violet-blue waters extended for at least four kilometers from shadowy bank to bank, with the ridge tapering to a point almost in its exact center.

Apparently, while they had been trekking along the elevation, the surrounding terrain, concealed from them by the dense and evil-minded vegetation, had imperceptibly taken off, leaving the ridge to become a peninsula that jutted out into the river. They seemed to be stranded. All they could do was retrace their steps and, since they had no idea how far back the split became part of the mainland again, the return journey might last almost as long as it had taken them to get there.

"I know we're heading in the right direction," Jrann-Pttt defended himself. "I wasn't aware of the river because we must have come by an overland route." Although he was telling the truth, at least insofar as he knew it himself, no one, not even Dfar-Lll, believed him.

"But let's rest a bit before we turn back," Mortland proposed, flopping to the ground. "I'm utterly used up."

"Maybe we don't need to go back," the vine said. "Not all the way, anyhow." Everyone stared. It waved its leaves brightly at them. "I notice the captain thoughtfully brought along lots of rope and there were scads of fallen logs just a bit back. Couldn't you just lash the logs together with the rope and make a—a thing on which we could float the rest of the way? On the water, you know."

The others continued to look at it open-mouthed.

"Just a little idea I had," it said modestly. "May not amount to much, but then you can't tell until you've tried, can you?"

"It—he—means a raft, I think," Mrs. Bernardi said.

Jrann-Pttt probed the raft concept in her mind, for he found the vegetable's mental processes curiously obscure. "What an excellent idea!" he exclaimed.

"It does not seem infeasible," Professor Bernardi admitted tightly. By now, he was suspicious of everyone and everything. *If I had never broached the idea of space travel to those peasants*, he thought, *I would be on Earth in the dubious comfort of my own home. That's what comes of trying to help humanity.*

*

"Well," observed the captain as the heavy raft hit the water with a tremendous splash, "she seems to be riverworthy." He rubbed his hands in anticipation, much of his surliness gone, now that he was about to deal with something he understood. "Since she is, in a manner of speaking, a ship, I suppose I assume command again?" He waited for objections, glancing involuntarily in Jrann-Pttt's direction.

There were none. "Right," he said, repressing any outward symptoms of relief.

He efficiently deployed the personnel to the positions on the raft where he felt they might be least useless, the gear being piled in the middle and surmounted by Algol, who naturally assumed possession of the softest and safest place by the divine right of cats.

The captain does have a commanding presence, Miss Anspacher thought, *and a sort of uncouth grace. Moreover, he cannot read my mind—in fact, he often cannot even understand me when I speak.*

"All right!" he bellowed. "Cast off!"

The vine unfastened the rope that it had insouciantly attached to a tree trunk, remarking to the others, "Don't let the trees intimidate you. Actually their bark is worse than their bite." Now it dropped lithely on board the raft, looking for a comfortable resting place.

"Please don't twine around me," Miss Anspacher said coldly. "If you insist upon coming with us, you will have to choose an inanimate object to cling to."

"All right, all right," it tried to soothe her. "No need to get yourself all worked up over such a mere triviality, is there? I'll just coil myself tidily around one of those spare logs. I must say you're warmer, though."

Yes, she is, isn't she? thought the captain, and squeezed her hand.

*

The raft drifted down the river. Since the current was flowing in the desired direction, there did not appear to be any need to use the poles, and everyone sat or reclined as comfortably as possible in the suffocating heat. The yellow haze had become so thick that they seemed to be at the bottom of a custard cup.

"I do hope we're heading the right way," Professor Bernardi said, *although who knows what is right and what is wrong any more?*

COLLECTOR'S ITEM

"Perhaps we aren't," Mrs. Bernardi mused, stroking Algol, who had crawled into her lap. "Perhaps we will go drifting along endlessly. Every sixteen days, it will get dark and every sixteen days it will get light, and meanwhile we will continue floating along, never going anywhere, never getting anywhere, never seeing anything but haze and raft and river and each other." Algol wheezed in his sleep.

"Nonsense!" Jrann-Pttt said rudely. "I have a compass. I know the direction perfectly well."

"And yet you let us think we were wandering about blindly." Miss Anspacher gave him a contemptuous look. The captain pressed her hand.

"Since you seem to breathe the same air and eat much the same food that we do, Mr. Pitt," Mrs. Bernardi changed her tack, "I suppose we'll be physically comfortable on your planet for the rest of our lives. Our children will be born there and our children's children, and eventually they'll forget all about Earth and think it was only a legend."

"But you did expect to settle permanently on Venus, didn't you?" the vine asked, bewilderedly. "Or for a long visit, anyway. So I don't really see that it makes much difference if you go to Jrann-Pttt's Alpha Centauri place. So much nicer to be living with friends, I should think."

"But Alpha Centauri is so very far away," Mrs. Bernardi sighed. "There wouldn't be much chance of our ever getting back."

"Look!" Mortland exclaimed. "The river's branching. Which fork do we take?"

*

Jrann-Pttt, who had been dabbling his arms idly in the translucent violet-blue water, withdrew them hastily as nine green eyes, obviously belonging to the same individual, rose to the surface and regarded him with more than casual interest. He consulted his compass. "Left."

"Contrarily!" the mosquito-bat suddenly squeaked, pointing a small rod at his companions. "Rightward."

There was a stunned silence.

"Monster!" Mortland cried in reproach. "You can talk! How could you deceive us like that?"

"Can talk," the creature retorted. "Me not intelligent life-form, ha! Who talks last talks best. Have not linguistic facility of inferior life-forms, but can communicate rudely in your language."

"Remember," Mortland cautioned, "there are ladies present."

"Have been lying low and laughing to self—ha, ha!—at witlessness of lowerly life-forms."

"But why?" Mrs. Bernardi demanded distractedly. "Haven't we been kind to you?"

"You be likewise well treated in our zoo," it assured her. "All of you. Our zoo finest in Galaxy. And clean, too."

"Now really, sir, I must protest—" Professor Bernardi began, trying to extricate a blaster unobtrusively from the pile of gear in which the too-confident terrestrials had cached their weapons.

Monster gestured with his rod. "This is lethal weapon. Do not try hindrancing me. Hate damage fine specimens. Captain, go rightward."

"Oh, is that so!" Greenfield retorted hotly. "Let me tell you, you—you insect!"

"George!" Miss Anspacher clutched his arm. "Do what it says. For my sake, George!"

"Oh, all right," he muttered. "Just for you, then. Told you not to trust any of 'em," he went on, reluctantly poling the raft in the ordered direction. "Foreigners!"

COLLECTOR'S ITEM

"Fine zoo," the mosquito-bat insisted. "Very clean. Run with utmost efficientness. Strict visiting hours."

*

"And there goes Plan D," the vine said lightly. There was a hint of laughter in its voice. Jrann-Pttt stared at it in consternation. "Are you also from the Alpha Centauri system, sir?" It turned its attention to the mosquito-bat. "Naturally I'm curious to know where I'm going," it explained, "since I seem definitely to be included in your gracious invitation."

"Alpha Centauri, hah!" the mosquito-bat snorted. "I from what Earthlets laughingly term Sirius. Alpha Centauri merely little star."

"Now see here!" Jrann-Pttt sprang to his feet. Criminal he might be, but he was not going to sit there and have his sun insulted!

"Gentlemen! Gentlemen!" Miss Anspacher cried. "No use getting yourself killed, Jrann-Pttt!"

"Correctly," Monster approved. "Elementary intelligence displayed. Why damage fine specimens?"

From one prison into another, the saurian mentalized bitterly.

Yes, returned Dfar-Lll, *and it's all your fault.* The junior lizard burst into tears. *I wish I had let Merglyt-Ruuu do what he wanted. I would have been better off.*

"Sirius," the vine repeated. "That's even farther away than Alpha Centauri, isn't it? I never thought I would get that far away from the swamp! This really will be an adventure!"

"How do you know—" Professor Bernardi began.

"Frankly," it went on, "I don't see why you chaps are so put out by the whole thing. What's the difference between Alpha Centauri and Sirius anyway? Matter of a few light-years, but otherwise a star's a star for all that."

"To Jrann-Pttt, we wouldn't have been specimens," Mrs. Bernardi said, belatedly recognizing the advantages of Alpha Centauri.

"No, not specimens," the vine told her easily. "I don't suppose you know he had no intention of taking you back to his system. He wanted you to help him kill the officers of his ship so they couldn't look for him and the other escaped prisoner or report back to his planet. Then he was going to put the ship out of commission and found his own colony here with you as his slaves. I'd just as soon be a specimen as a slave. Sooner. Better to reign in a zoo than serve in a swamp!"

"Just how do you know all this?" Miss Anspacher demanded.

"It's obvious enough," Bernardi said gloomily. "Another telepath." *How can we compete or even cope with creatures like these? What a fool I was to think I could outwit them.*

"Telepathy just tricksomeness," the mosquito-bat put in jealously. "I have no telepathy, yet superior to all."

"But why should Mr. Pitt want to kill his officers?" Mrs. Bernardi asked querulously. "He's the commandant, isn't he? Or is he a professor? I never got that straight."

"He was one of the criminals on the ship," the vine told her. "What you might call a confidence man. This is about the only system in the Galaxy where he isn't wanted. He did tell you the truth, though, when he said they were sent on an expedition to collect zoological specimens. Dangerous work," it sighed, "and so his people use criminals for it. They were sent out in small detachments. Our friend here killed his guard in a fight over a female prisoner, which was why—"

"But what happened to the female prisoner?" Miss Anspacher's eye caught Dfar-Lll's. "Oh, no!" she gasped.

COLLECTOR'S ITEM

"Why not?" Dfar-Lll demanded. "I'm as much of a female as you are. Maybe even more."

The captain leaned close to Miss Anspacher. "No one can be more feminine than you are, Dolores," he whispered.

"But he—she's so young!" Mrs. Bernardi wailed.

The vine made an amused sound. "Don't you have juvenile delinquents on Earth?"

"Oh, what does all that matter now?" Jrann-Pttt said sullenly. "We're all going to a Sirian zoo, anyway."

"Correctly," approved the monster-bat. "Finest zoo. Clean. Commodious cages. Reasonable visiting hours. Very nice."

Mrs. Bernardi began to cry.

"Now," the vine comforted her, "a zoo's not so bad. After all, most of us spend our lives in cages of one kind or another, and without the basic security a zoo affords—"

"But we don't know we're in cages," Mrs. Bernardi sobbed. "That's the important thing."

Professor Bernardi looked at the vine. "But why are you—" he began, then halted. "Perhaps I don't want an answer," he said. There was no hope at all left in him, now that there was no doubt.

"You are wise," the vine agreed quietly. Algol arose from Mr. Bernardi's lap and rubbed against its thick pale green stem. He knew. The mosquito-bat looked at both of them restlessly.

The yellow haze had deepened to old gold. Now it was beginning to turn brown.

"It's twilight," Miss Anspacher observed. "Soon it will be dark."

"Perhaps we'll sail right past his ship in the night," Mortland suggested hopefully.

The mosquito-bat gave a snort. "Ship has lights. All modern convenients."

Suddenly the air seemed to have grown chilly—colder than it had any right to be on that torrid planet. All around them, it was dark and very quiet.

"I think I do see lights," Mortland said.

"Must be ship," Monster replied. And somehow the rest of them could sense the uneasiness in the thin, piping, alien voice. "Must be!"

"Your ship's a very large one then," Bernardi commented as they rounded a bend and a whole colony of varicolored pastel lights sprang up ahead of them.

"Not my ship!" the mosquito-bat exclaimed in a voice pierced with anguish. "Not my ship!"

Before them rose the fantastic, twisting, convoluting, turning spires of a tall, marvelous, glittering city.

"You will find that the streets actually are filled with chlorophyll," the vine said. "And I know you'll be happy here, all of you. You see, we can't have you going back to your planets now. No matter how good your intentions were, you'd destroy us. You do see that, don't you?"

"You may be right," Bernardi agreed dispiritedly, "although that doesn't cheer us any. But what will you do with us?"

"You'll be provided with living quarters comparable to those on your own planets," the vine told him, "and you'll give lectures just as if you were in a university—only you'll be much more secure. I assure you—" its voice was very gentle now—"you'll hardly know you're in a zoo."

www.ingramcontent.com/pod-product-compliance
Lightning Source LLC
Chambersburg PA
CBHW050908120626
46554CB00003B/1069